My Grandma's Dog

Written and Designed by Versey A Williams
Illustrations by Karen Rose Shinaver

Illustrations by Karen Rose Shinaver

Narrated by Deon K. Williams

Soft cover published by AuthorHouse.
ISBN: 1-4184-9055-5(sc)

A Christian Bible Studies Publication
www.ChristianStudies7.com

Printed in the United States of America
Color House Graphics, Grand Rapids, MI
October 2004

To Sharon Elizabeth,
the inspiration behind this little story.

And

To all the hearts, big and small,
who need a little more joy.

This is a story about our dog. Her name is Nala.

Nala is not an ordinary dog. She is a special dog.

She is my Grandma's dog.

Nala has been in our family for a long time.
Her birthday is February 9, 1998.

She was smaller than her brothers and sisters.

I was a little boy when Nala came to live with my Dad and me.

Nala played with me all of the time.
She is my friend.

She helped my Dad tuck me in at night.
She said my prayers with me too.

Nala grew and I grew. Nala used to be taller than me.

Now I am taller than Nala.

One day my Poppee decided that he did not want to
be married to my Grandma anymore.

She was alone and very sad.

One day we decided to go and visit Grandma.
Nala had never been inside of Grandma's house before.

She saw how sad Grandma was.
She wanted Grandma to feel better.
So she went over to Grandma and laid her head on her lap.

Grandma smiled again.

Nala decided to move in with Grandma.

Grandma was very glad.

Now Nala and Grandma have lots of fun together.
Nala makes Grandma smile a lot.

She laughs too and gives Nala lots of hugs around her neck!

Nala used to be my Dad's dog and mine.

Now she is my Grandma's dog.

But Grandma shares.

When Nala came to live with Grandma, she did not have a bed.

So Grandma went shopping.

Grandma laid on every bed to make sure it would be just right.
Bed after bed, after bed.

Grandma finally found just the right one.
It was very soft. Just right for Nala.

Grandma tucked Nala in every night until she got used to her new bed.

Nala doesn't always sleep in her new bed.

She sleeps with Grandma.

Grandma never cooked for a dog before.

She was a little mixed up at first.

She gave Nala food from her dinner plates.

Then my Dad told her that Nala really needed to eat her
own kind of food in her own bowl.

Now she eats dog food. Grandma bought her new dinner
bowls and a doggy place mat to match the kitchen.

Nala used to be me and my Dad's dog.

Now she is my Grandma's dog.

Nala likes being outdoors.

She can open the patio screen door.

But she can't close it back.

Grandma and Nala play together. Grandma likes Frisbee.

Nala likes to jump for butterflies.

Grandma just can't jump like she used to.

Grandma loves flowers. They are beautiful.

Sometimes there isn't enough room for Nala and Grandma's flowers.

Nala is bigger than Grandma's flowers.
But Grandma doesn't mind.

One time Grandma was working in her flower garden.

She looked up and saw Nala on the other side of the fence.

Nala did not know how to come back through the fence.

Grandma always helps Nala.

So she helped Nala back through the fence.
But when she tried to climb back over the fence, she got stuck.

Nala did not know what to do.
Neither did Grandma.

Bath time is fun at Grandm'a house.

There are lots of bubbles!

Nala jumps out of the bathtub
and runs through the house!

Then Grandma tries to brush her hair.

Grandma can't jump that high but she's a pretty good runner!

One time Nala left home without asking Grandma first.

Grandma was worried about Nala. She called the police for help.
"Help" Grandma said. "My dog is lost."

Grandma called my Dad too. My Dad found Nala
a few blocks from home. Boy was she in trouble!

Nala ran off with one of her friends. They played in the weeds.
She was dirty and her hair had little twigs all over it.
Grandma doesn't like us to get dirty.

Grandma was happy to have Nala back but she still made her
take a bath. Nala never goes in her dog house. But she did that day.

Nala doesn't leave home anymore without
asking Grandma first.

Nala likes to bury her bones in the dirt.
Her nose gets dirty.

Grandma doesn't like dirty noses.

Then Nala digs them back up and brings them in the house.
Grandma doesn't like dirt in the house.

One day she washed Nala's bone for her.

Nala did not like washed bones. But she did let Grandma
clean her nose. And still does.

Grandma has a lot more rules than Dad did.
But Nala doesn't mind.

Grandma and Nala do lots of things together.
They are best friends.

Nala takes Grandma for a walk almost everyday.
Grandma says they have to watch their weight.

One morning it was very cold.
Grandma and Nala could not take their walk.
Nala did not have a coat.

So Grandma went shopping.
She could not find a coat or
a sweater that Nala would like.

So Grandma gave Nala one of her warmest sweaters.
Nala didn't like it but she wore it anyway.

Then Dad told Grandma that Nala already had a coat.
Grandma never had to dress a dog before.

Nala comes to visit my classroom at school.
Since she can't drive, Grandma brings her.

Nala has very good manners.

Nala and Grandma spend lots of time together.

Sometimes on the deck . . . . .

in the sunroom . . . .

even in front of the fireplace.

Since Nala came to live with Grandma, she isn't sad anymore.

Grandma even took her to the Hallelujah Party at church!

Nala went as a dog.

Grandma really loves Nala.
She calls Nala her baby.

Sometimes she calls Nala her honeygirl.

One time Nala got an ouchy.
Her leg was broken.
She hurt very bad.
Nala couldn't walk.
Nala was very scared.

Grandma took her to the dog hospital.
She had a lady and a man doctor.
She had a man and lady nurse too.

Nala had to spend the night in the dog hospital.
They tried to make her feel better.

But Grandma made her feel the best.

Grandma really loves her dog.

She is not just an ordinary dog.

She is my Grandma's dog.

Sometimes people are afraid of Nala. She has big teeth.
As big as her smile.

She protects my Grandma.
And my Grandma protects Nala.

When Nala gets in trouble with my Dad,
she runs to Grandma!

Nala likes to sit on my Grandma's lap.

Nala is bigger than Grandma's lap.

Nala helps Grandma with everything!

They clean the house . . . .

They do laundry . . . .

They answer the door   . . .

They even play the piano!

Nala likes riding in Grandma's car.
Grandma opens the sunroof for her.
She catches the wind with her nose!

Grandma's heart feels much better!

And Nala is happy too!

Nala doesn't like it when Grandma has to go on a trip.

My Dad and me are not as much fun as Grandma is.
Nala misses Grandma when she has to go away.

Sometimes Nala has to go to the dog sitter.
Grandma never had to get a dog sitter before.
Grandma looked and looked and looked.

Finally Grandma found just the right place.
"The Dog Hotel".
Grandma takes some of her toys and a
blanket so she won't be homesick.

Grandma always calls back to see how Nala is doing.
Grandma misses Nala too.

They are both very happy when Grandma comes back to get her!

Nala is my Grandma's Dog.

Nala takes care of Grandma.
And Grandma takes care of Nala.
Sometimes it is just the two of them.

Nala is not an ordinary dog. She is a special dog.
She is my Grandma's gift from God.

Sometimes things will happen that can make us sad.

But God can make it better.

About my Grandson
This is my grandson's 9th year birthday present. He, Nala and I have had countless adventures together! No one can tell the stories quite the way that he can.

About Nala
Nala is a pedigreed Rottweiler. Her mother's name is Lovely and her father's name is Taz. My son brought her home when my grandson was two years old and Nala was just three months old.

About Karen
Karen Rose Shinaver is now a senior at Michigan State University double majoring in computer science and studio art. She has been a joy to work with. She made all of my ideas come alive! Her future plans are to create video games, either designing or programming them. She also plans to get a puppy of her own!

About Versey
In my work as pastor and Board Certified Chaplain, I am priviledged to share in both the joy and pain of people's lives. It was through my own pain and brokenness that My Grandma's Dog came to be. It is a true story that begins with grief and ends with a peace and contentment which I have never known. Nala has been my closest human example of unconditional love - yes I know that Nala really is a dog. But she's my dog!

It is really true that all things work out for the good when we open ourselves to God's blessings. My divorce was only a mild thing when we look at the suffering others must contend with and in comparison to some of the many heartaches I have experienced throughout my life. However, this time was different. God gave me a little something to share with all of you.

Life brings unplanned twists and turns - so to all of the hearts, big and small, I hope My Grandma's Dog will give you a bit more joy and hope for your future.